YAFFA GANZ

MY BOOK

Growing Up
With Family and Friends

Illustrated by Liat Benyamini Ariel

To
Binyamin Zev ben Bezalel ע"ה
and to
Yishai ben Tovya Yair ע"ה

New links on an old and sacred chain;
new leaves on an ancient and hallowed tree.
May you grow and multiply and be blessed.

FIRST EDITION
First Impression … December 1993
Second Impression … November 1997

Published and Distributed by
MESORAH PUBLICATIONS, Ltd. / Brooklyn, N.Y 11232

Distributed in Israel by SIFRIATI / A. GITLER — BOOKS
10 Hashomer Street / Bnei Brak 51361

Distributed in Australia and New Zealand by GOLD'S BOOK & GIFT SHOP
36 William Street / Balaclava 3183, Vic., Australia

Distributed in South Africa by KOLLEL BOOKSHOP
22 Muller Street / Yeoville 2198, Johannesburg, South Africa

THE ARTSCROLL YOUTH SERIES®
MY BOOK – GROWING UP WITH FAMILY AND FRIENDS
© *Copyright 1993 by* MESORAH PUBLICATIONS, LTD. *and* YAFFA GANZ
4401 Second Avenue / Brooklyn, N.Y. 11232 / (718) 921-9000

Typography by Compuscribe at ArtScroll Studios, Ltd.
4401 Second Avenue / Brooklyn, N.Y. 11232 / (718) 921-9000

Printed in the United States of America by Edison Lithographing and Printing
Custom bound by Sefercraft, Inc. / 4401 Second Avenue / Brooklyn N.Y. 11232

This Book
Belongs to:
every one

ᦥ Introduction

On the sixth day of creation, G-d created Man — the only man in the entire world. His name was Adam. But G-d thought that it was not good for Adam to be alone, and so He made him a helpmate to stand at his side. Her name was Chava. Together, Adam and Chava would build and guard the world for future generations.

Since then, no man or woman or child has ever been alone. Everyone is blessed with someone — parents, grandparents or great-grandparents; brothers or sisters; uncles, aunts, cousins or friends. Together, we all give, take, help, love, build and create.

The Torah teaches us that every person in the world is unique and priceless because each and every human being is created in the Image of G-d. That's why every newborn baby is such a wonderful, irreplaceable gift.

But when you were born, you were two gifts rolled into one, and your birth was the occasion of a double simcha. Not only were you welcomed as the newest member of your own private family; you were welcomed into Am Yisrael — the Jewish people — as well.

Of all the many peoples in the world, G-d chose one — the Jewish people — to be His own special nation. He gave them His Torah and commanded them to be a Mamleches Kohanim and a Goy Kadosh — a Kingdom of Priests and a Holy Nation. Every Jewish child is a new link in the long chain of holy people who stood at Mount Sinai; each is a new leaf on an ancient tree whose roots go back more than 3700 years, all the way to Avraham Avinu, the first Jew.

By the time you reach your bar or bas mitzvah, the pages of this book will be full of photos, information and fond memories. I hope that each and every one will help you remember who you are and where you came from, and will help you plan where you want to go during your life.

May your journey be filled with Torah and mitzvos, kindness, love and good deeds. And may you be a source of Jewish blessing and joy for your parents and your people — from the day of your birth v'ahd meah v'esrim – until you are at least one hundred and twenty years old!

Sincerely,
Yaffa Ganz

מזל טוב!

Mazal Tov!

A Baby Is Born!

On _March_,

the _____ day in the Hebrew month of _____

in the Hebrew year _____ [_____ , 19__]

in the city of _New York_

at _____ o'clock,

at the _Beth page_ hospital

I was born to _bear_ and _goodgril_

Here I Am:

[Photo of baby]

I was the **litel** child in our family;

the **frist** grandchild in my father's family;

and the **five** grandchild in my mother's family.

My mother said I looked like: **an babt**

My father said I looked like: **an elepant**

IT'S A BOY!

ישימך אלקים כְּאפרים וכמנשֶׁה

Shalom Zachor

The first Shabbos evening after my birth, my parents made a Shalom Zachor. It was Shabbos Parashas _____.

My Bris Milah

קיים את הילד הזה לאביו ולאמו ויקרא שמו בישראל

My Bris Milah took place on: _____

It took place at: _____

The name of the mohel was: _____

I was given the name:

_____

Explanation of my name: _____

כשם שנכנס לברית כן יכנס לתורה ולחופה ולמעשים טובים!

Pidyon Haben

As a firstborn son (whose parents are neither Kohanim nor Leviim), I had a Pidyon Haben when I was thirty days old.

The date was: _____

The Kohein who redeemed me was: _____

IT'S A GIRL!

יְשִׂימֵךְ אֱלֹקִים כְּשָׂרָה רִבְקָה רָחֵל וְלֵאָה:

Girls are given a name in the synagogue on a Monday, Thursday or Shabbos, the first time the Torah is read after their birth.

I was named on: _____

at: _____

מִי שֶׁבֵּרַךְ אֲבוֹתֵינוּ אַבְרָהָם יִצְחָק וְיַעֲקֹב... וַיִּקְרָא שְׁמָהּ בְּיִשְׂרָאֵל

I was given the name:
_____

Explanation of my name: _____

My family made a Kiddush/Zeved Habat in my honor

on _____

at _____

Our Family Tree

בינו שנות ודור ודור

Today I am the newest leaf
on our family tree.
Our family is thousands of years old.
The roots in our tree go all the way back
to Avraham Avinu.
But this picture-tree only goes back four generations,
to my great grandparents.

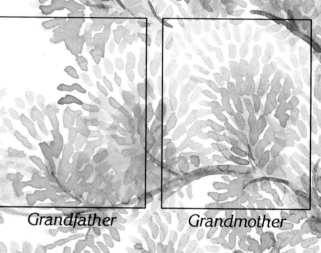

Mother

Grandfather

Grandmother

Great-Grandfather

Great-Grandmother

Great-Grandfather

Great-Grandmother

Me

Father

Grandfather

Grandmother

Great-Grandfather

Great-Grandmother

Great-Grandfather

Great-Grandmother

My Mother's Parents

שאל אביך ויגדך

My grandfather's name is: _____

He was named after: _____

He comes from: _____

He was born on: _____

He works (worked) as: _____

My name for him is: _____

The thing I like best about him is: _____

My grandmother's name is: _____

Her maiden name was: _____

She was named after: _____

She comes from: _____

She was born on: _____

She works (worked) as: _____

My name for her is: _____

The thing I like best about her is: _____

My Father's Parents
זקניך ויאמרו לך

My grandfather's name is: _____

He was named after: _____

He comes from: _____

He was born on: _____

He works (worked) as: _____

My name for him is: _____

The thing I like best about him is: _____

My grandmother's name is: _____

Her maiden name was: _____

She was named after: _____

She comes from: _____

She was born on: _____

She works (worked) as: _____

My name for her is: _____

The thing I like best about her is: _____

My Parents

All About My Father
שמע בני מוסר אביך

My father's name is: _____

He was born in: _____

His birthday is: _____

He was named after: _____

He studied at: _____

He works as: _____

Things my father likes to do: _____

Things I like to do with my father: _____

All About My Mother
ואל תטוש תורת אמך

My mother's name is: _____

She was born in: _____

Her birthday is: _____

She was named after: _____

She studied at: _____

She works as: _____

Things my mother likes to do: _____

Things I like to do with my mother: _____

My Parents at Their Wedding
קול חתן וקול כלה

[photo]

My parents were married on:

_____

They were married at:

_____

Our Family Today

בֵּית נֶאֱמָן בְּיִשְׂרָאֵל

[photo]

My Brothers and Sisters

וְהִרְבָּה אַרְבֶּה אֶת זַרְעֶךָ

Name	Birthday
_____	_____
_____	_____
_____	_____
_____	_____
_____	_____
_____	_____
_____	_____
_____	_____
_____	_____

Important Family Dates

זכור ימות עולם

Birthdays

Name	Hebrew Date	English Date

Anniversaries

Occasion	Hebrew Date	English Date

Other Occasions

Occasion	Hebrew Date	English Date

Aunts, Uncles, Cousins
on My Father's Side

Uncle _____   Aunt _____

Cousins _____   _____

_____   _____

_____   _____

Uncle _____   Aunt _____

Cousins _____   _____

_____   _____

_____   _____

Uncle _____   Aunt _____

Cousins _____   _____

_____   _____

_____   _____

Uncle _____   Aunt _____

Cousins _____   _____

_____   _____

_____   _____

Uncle _____   Aunt _____

Cousins _____   _____

_____   _____

_____   _____

Aunts, Uncles, Cousins
on My Mother's Side

Uncle _Steven_ Aunt _Hillary_

Cousins _Eli_ _Osh_

Rebecca

Uncle _____ Aunt _____

Cousins _____

_____

_____

Uncle _____ Aunt _____

Cousins _____

_____

_____

Uncle _____ Aunt _____

Cousins _____

_____

_____

Uncle _____ Aunt _____

Cousins _____

_____

_____

Firsts

I first turned over when I was _____ weeks old.

I first smiled when I was _____ weeks old.

I first sat by myself when I was _____ months old.

I first stood by myself when I was _____ months old.

I took my first step when I was _____ months old.

ברוך ה' יום יום

More Firsts

Words, Brachos, Tefillos
מפי עוללים ויונקים יסדת עוז

When I was _____ months old, I said my first word.
It was:_____

When I was _____ years old, I said my first bracha.
It was:_____

When I was _____ years old, I learned my first tefilla.
It was:_____

When I was _____ years old, I learned my first song.
It was:_____

Here is a list of the first twenty words I learned to say:

_____ _____ _____ _____

_____ _____ _____ _____

_____ _____ _____ _____

_____ _____ _____ _____

_____ _____ _____ _____

Progress

[photo]

This is what I looked like when I was three months old.

[photo]

This is what I looked like when I was six months old.

 # *Progress*

[photo]

This is what I looked like when I was nine months old.

[photo]

This is what I look like now.
As you can see, I'm progressing!

My First Birthday

I'm not a newborn baby anymore! There are lots of things I can do – roll over and smile and sit up by myself. And soon b'ezras Hashem I'll be doing lots more. I'm getting bigger day by day! My parents are very happy. Me too.

This is me on my first birthday.

My father said:

_____

_____

_____

_____

_____

My mother said:

_____

_____

_____

_____

I didn't say anything at all. I just laughed!

My Second Birthday

I'm two years old!

[photo]

You can't imagine how much I've learned in two years. I can walk and talk and eat by myself. Everyone likes to play with me. I like to play with them too!

My mother thinks I am _____

My father thinks I am_____

My Third Birthday

Today is a special birthday. I am three years old. Old enough to say a bracha by myself. Old enough to help my mother or father. Old enough to light Shabbos candles with my mother or Chanukah candles with my father. Almost old enough to go to school and learn Torah! Here is a picture of me at my third birthday party.

[photo]

This is how we celebrated:

_____

_____

Some families celebrate a boy's third birthday with an *opsharin* — a first haircut. My *opsharin* was on _____.

My mother hopes that when I grow up I will _____

_____

My father hopes that when I grow up I will _____

_____

My First Day at Kindergarten

תורה צוה לנו משה

Today I began kindergarten!

The name of my school is:

_____

My teacher's name is:

_____

Here I am!

[photo]

But this is only the beginning. B'ezras Hashem, I'm going to learn to read and write, to say all of the brachos, to daven all of the tefillos, and to learn as much of Hashem's Torah as I possibly can. Every single day for the rest of my life!

First Grade

ראשית חכמה יראת ה'

This is me in first grade.

[photo]

The name of my school is:

_____

My teacher's name is:

_____

This is how my mother described my first day at school:

_____

I received my first siddur in _____ grade.

I received my first chumash in _____ grade.

Eighth Grade

חנוך לנער על פי דרכו

How quickly the time has passed!
I'm in my last year in elementary school.
Next year I'll be learning at the _____
yeshiva/day school.

So far, my favorite teachers were:

_____

_____

My favorite subjects were:

_____

_____

The nicest thing that ever happened to me in school was:

_____

_____

This is a picture of my graduating class.

(photo)

כל ישראל חברים!
All Jews Are Friends!

[photo]

Summers With My Family

Summertime is special time — time to spend with my family. Here are some of the things our family has done together during the summers.

We've gone to:

My favorite place was:

What I liked best of all was:

Summer Pictures of My Family

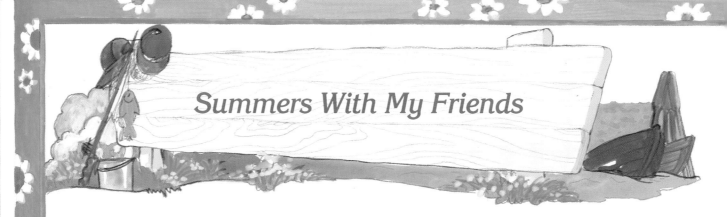

Summers With My Friends

Summers are for friends too. Last summer I: _____

_____

_____

_____

The thing I like best about the summer is: _____

_____

_____

_____

_____

My favorite summer camp was: _____

My favorite counselor's name was: _____

The most interesting thing we did at camp was: _____

_____

_____

_____

Summer Pictures of My Friends

The Land of Israel

ונתתי את הארץ הזאת לזרעך אחריך אחזת עולם

Eretz Yisrael is the most important place in the world. It is the Land which G-d gave to the Jewish people forever. It is the only Land where the Beis Hamikdash can be built. Someday, all the Jews in the world will return to the Land of Israel. I hope to get there as soon as possible!

The first thing I'll want to see is:_____

_____

_____

_____

Then I'll go to: _____

_____

_____

_____

The first person in our family who went to Israel was:

_____

Pictures From Israel

Bas Mitzvah

בת שתים עשרה למצוות

(photo)

Today I am 12. I am bas mitzvah, a Daughter of the Commandments.

Today I am obligated to observe the laws in Hashem's Torah, just like my mother.

The date of my bas mitzvah is the Hebrew date of my twelfth birthday: _____

Bas mitzvah means being a bas Torah. It means being responsible for keeping the mitzvos. It means learning Torah so that I will know how to act and what to do. Here's what I learned about in preparation for my bas mitzvah: _____

_____

_____

_____

This is what I do differently now that I am bas mitzvah:

_____

_____

_____

_____

_____

_____

And here's how our family marked the occasion:

_____

_____

_____

_____

Bar Mitzvah

בן שלש עשרה למצוות

(photo)

Today I am 13. I am a bar mitzvah, a Son of the Commandments. Today I am obligated to keep the laws in Hashem's Torah, just like my father.

The date of my bar mitzvah is: _____

The parasha of the week is: _____

The first day I put on tefillin was: _____

Bar mitzvah means being a ben Torah. It means being responsible for keeping the mitzvos. It means learning Torah so that I will know how to act and what to do.

Here's what I learned about in preparation for my bar mitzvah:

_____

_____

_____

_____

And here's how our family marked the occasion:

_____

_____

_____

_____

מזל וברכה

Autographs, Good Wishes and Blessings
From People I Love

Things to Remember
About My Family

והגדת לבנך ביום ההוא

Here are some of the things I want to remember about our family. Someday, b'ezras Hashem, I'll tell them to *my* children.

_____

_____

_____

_____

_____

_____

_____

_____

_____

_____

_____

_____

Things to Remember

**About Am Yisrael
and the Torah**

וְהָגִיתָ בּוֹ יוֹמָם וָלַיְלָה

Here are some important things I want to remember for myself –
things which might help me become a better person and a better Jew.

Things to Think About for the Future
דע ... לאן אתה הולך

Now that I am bar/bas mitzvah, there are many important things to think about for the future, things I didn't have to think about before, when I was younger. Here are just a few

_____

_____

_____

_____

_____

_____

_____

_____

עד מאה ועשרים!